A 20th Century Fox Presents

ANASTAS

A Don Bluth / Gary Goldman Film

Adapted by Nancy Krulik
Illustrated by the Thompson Brothers

 A GOLDEN BOOK • NEW YORK

Golden Books Publishing Company, Inc., New York, New York 10106

Long ago there was a beautiful princess who lived in an enchanted world of palaces and grand parties. Her name was Anastasia Romanov. She was the youngest daughter in the Russian royal family and the apple of her grandmother's eye.

Anastasia's grandmother, Empress Marie, lived far away, in Paris. Anastasia missed her dearly. But the empress had given her granddaughter something to remember her by—a music box that played a beautiful lullaby. Anastasia wore the flower-shaped key to the box around her neck and thought of her grandmother whenever she listened to the music.

One day, while the empress was visiting from Paris, an evil man named Rasputin ordered his guards to tear down the palace gates. Rasputin had a reliquary, a container filled with powerful minions who obeyed his every command. Almost all the Romanovs were captured. Only Anastasia and her grandmother escaped—thanks to a quick-thinking servant boy, Dimitri, who led them through a secret doorway to freedom.

As Anastasia and her grandmother made their escape across a frozen river, Rasputin jumped from a bridge to stop them. The ice broke, and Rasputin tried to drown the princess in the river below. But Anastasia pulled free of his grasp—and Rasputin drowned instead. The evil man disappeared into the underworld below.

Anastasia and her grandmother ran for the train to Paris. But just as they were about to board, Anastasia fell and hit her head—and the two became separated.

After the Russian Revolution, it was thought that the Romanovs had all been killed. But a rumor that Anastasia might still be alive spread throughout Russia and Europe.

The story made its way to Paris, and to Empress Marie herself. She offered a reward of ten million rubles to anyone who could find her beloved granddaughter. For more than ten years, the old woman met with girls claiming to be the princess. But the real Anastasia could not be found.

One determined pair of schemers, Dimitri, the servant boy, and his friend Vladimir, were certain they had what it took to fool the empress—the music box given to Anastasia by her grandmother. Dimitri had found it in the palace after the battle. Now, they figured, all they needed was to find a girl who looked like Anastasia.

One day, a poor orphan girl named Anya and her puppy, Pooka, arrived
on the steps of the deserted palace. Anya had been told that Dimitri could
be found there, and that he could help her get to Paris. Anya desperately
wanted to go because her only clue to her past was an inscription on the
key she wore around her neck. It read, TOGETHER IN PARIS.

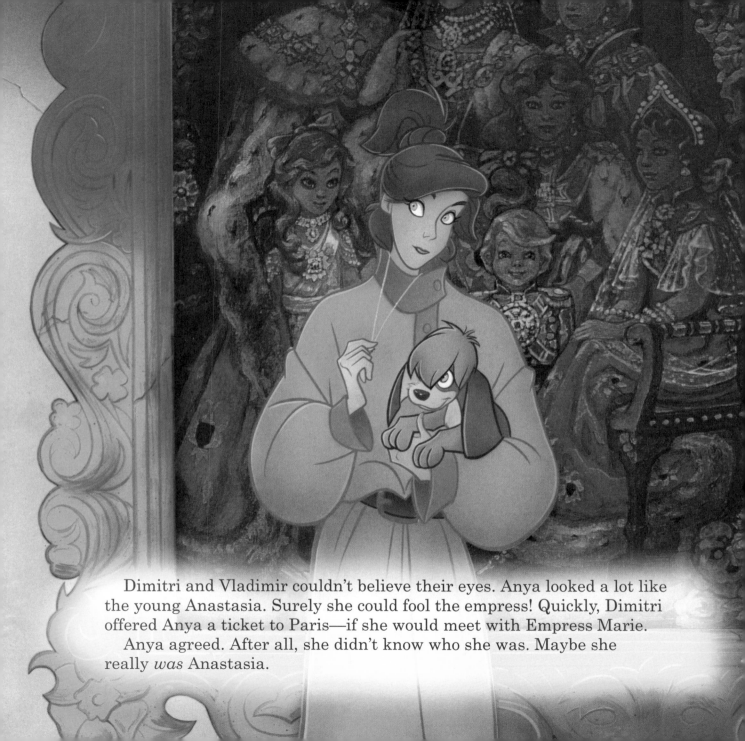

Dimitri and Vladimir couldn't believe their eyes. Anya looked a lot like the young Anastasia. Surely she could fool the empress! Quickly, Dimitri offered Anya a ticket to Paris—if she would meet with Empress Marie.

Anya agreed. After all, she didn't know who she was. Maybe she really *was* Anastasia.

If Anya was going to convince the empress, she would have to learn everything there was to know about the Romanovs. So, as they traveled by train and ship to Paris, Dimitri and Vladimir taught Anya all about Anastasia. They also coached her on how to eat, speak, and dance like a princess. Dimitri even taught Anya how to waltz.

Meanwhile, even from his distant home in the underworld, Rasputin could see the resemblance between Anya and Anastasia. And Rasputin wanted the girl dead!

So one night, as Anya slept, Rasputin entered her dreams and convinced her to sleepwalk off the side of the ship. Luckily, Dimitri awoke and rescued Anya just as she was about to plunge into the sea!

When they got to Paris, Vladimir and Dimitri dressed Anya in a beautiful gown and took her to the opera. They knew the empress would be there that evening. But the empress refused to meet Anya. She had seen too many Anastasia imitations before.

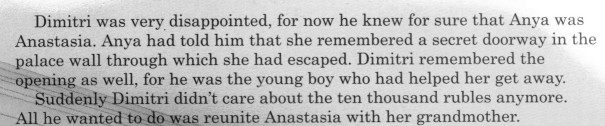

Dimitri was very disappointed, for now he knew for sure that Anya was Anastasia. Anya had told him that she remembered a secret doorway in the palace wall through which she had escaped. Dimitri remembered the opening as well, for he was the young boy who had helped her get away.

Suddenly Dimitri didn't care about the ten thousand rubles anymore. All he wanted to do was reunite Anastasia with her grandmother.

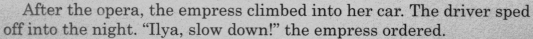

After the opera, the empress climbed into her car. The driver sped off into the night. "Ilya, slow down!" the empress ordered.

But the driver was not Ilya, her chauffeur. It was Dimitri! He stopped the car outside the place where Anya was staying and handed the music box to the empress. "It's just possible that she's been as lost and alone as you," he said softly.

Tears welled in the old woman's eyes as she looked at the familiar music box.

Carrying the music box, the empress bravely went to Anya's room. "Who exactly are you?" she asked the girl.

Anya fiddled nervously with the flower-shaped key around her neck. "I was hoping *you* could tell *me*," she replied quietly.

The empress asked for the necklace and placed the key in the music box. The box began to play a lullaby that they both remembered. Anya was the real Princess Anastasia!

Anastasia's safe return became the talk of Paris and all of Europe.
Word even spread to the underworld—and to Rasputin.

He was overjoyed. He could finally finish off the last of the Romanovs!
Rasputin grabbed his reliquary and prepared to reenter the mortal world.

Just as a ball in Anastasia's honor was about to begin, the princess ran into the Tuillerie Gardens to look for Pooka. Rasputin suddenly appeared. "I am Rasputin, destroyed by your despicable family!" he snarled. "What goes around, comes around. No one can help you!"

"Wanna bet?"

Anastasia turned in the direction of a familiar voice. It was Dimitri! He had come to her rescue once again, but he was no match for Rasputin and his evil minions. They blasted Dimitri high in the air and dropped him on the back of a stone statue of Pegasus, the flying horse.

"Kill him!" Rasputin ordered.

The Pegasus statue sprang to life and, bucking upward, tossed Dimitri from its back. He fell lifeless to the ground.

Anastasia was heartbroken. She lunged angrily at Rasputin.
The evil man was surprised, but he stood his ground. He grabbed
his reliquary and shot a stream of minions in Anastasia's direction.
She fell to the ground in pain.

Pooka, Anastasia's loyal canine companion,
sensed that his friend was in trouble. So he leaped
up and snatched Rasputin's reliquary from his hands.
Without the reliquary, Rasputin was powerless. The
minions disappeared in a cloud of smoke.

Pooka dropped the reliquary near Anastasia's feet.
"This is for my family," she declared as she stomped it to
bits, "and for Dimitri!"

Kaboom! The reliquary exploded in a flash of light. Rasputin's screams filled the night as his skin glowed. Then, catching fire, the evil man melted and turned to dust, which blew away into the wind.

Anastasia hurried over to Dimitri, who lay as still as death. The princess's eyes welled with tears as she stroked the young man's hair. Then, suddenly, Dimitri let out a small moan. He was alive!

Anastasia looked from Dimitri's eyes to the party being held in her honor. She knew that Dimitri would never fit in with her grandmother's high-society friends. She had to choose between true love and her role as a princess. . . .

Anastasia knew that her grandmother would want her
to follow her heart. So that is exactly what she did.